BUNKED!
The Musical

Book and Lyrics
by Alaina Kunin
and Bradford Proctor

Music by
Bradford Proctor

A SAMUEL FRENCH ACTING EDITION

SAMUEL FRENCH
FOUNDED 1830
NEW YORK HOLLYWOOD LONDON TORONTO
SAMUELFRENCH.COM

ISBN 978-0-573-69968-9   Printed in U.S.A.   #28025

RENTAL MATERIALS

An orchestration consisting of **Piano/Conductor Score** will be loaned two months prior to the production ONLY on the receipt of the Licensing Fee quoted for all performances, the rental fee and a refundable deposit.

Please contact Samuel French for perusal of the music materials as well as a performance license application.

IMPORTANT BILLING AND CREDIT
REQUIREMENTS

BUNKED!: THE MUSICAL was first produced by the New York International Fringe Festival in New York City on August 17, 2010. The performance was directed by Seth Sikes, with sets by Paul DePoo, costumes by Sasha Richter, sound by Janie Bullard, and lighting by Matt Taylor. The Production Stage Manager was Karen Evanouskas. The cast was as follows:

ANABEL. . . . . .Amanda Jane Cooper

OLIVER. . . . . .Tim Ehrlich

MAX . . . . .Jake Loewenthal

STEWART . . . . .Ben Moss

CARMEN . . . . Lizzie Klemperer

CHARACTERS

All must look believably 18. Ideally, the show should be multi-ethnic.

Females:

ANABEL – Nerdy, bookish, very quirky girl, Oliver's sister (need not look alike) and love interest for Stewart. Very likable in a geeky, mousy kind of way. Pop soprano, must have strong belt and mix.

CARMEN – Strong, brassy city girl who makes perhaps the biggest emotional journey at camp. Love interest for Max. Must be able to play both sassiness and vulnerability. Pop alto or soprano, must have a strong belt.

Males:

MAX – The golden boy with a heart to match, whose summer plans are thrown for a loop when a secret is revealed. Love interest for Carmen. Must be very likeable in an earthy, wholesome kind of way. Pop baritone/tenor.

STEWART – Confused and directionless dreamer, he spends the summer searching for what he is going to do with his life. Bisexual, a love interest for both Anabel and Oliver (must be believably straight or gay). Pop tenor.

OLIVER – The openly gay teenage boy (but not stereotypically gay) who wants to be the center of attention, yearning to make it in the big city. Anabel's adopted brother (need not look alike) and gay love interest for Stewart. Pop tenor.

Other:

LOUDSPEAKER – Male, this can be a pre-recorded role, a spunky, sassy voice piped over the loudspeaker of the camp. Note: The counselors often remark how the loudspeaker sounds a bit gay.

AUTHOR'S NOTES

If any pop culture references/slang terms are no longer in use, please feel free to update them at your discretion!

MUSICAL NUMBERS

Best Summer Ever..ALL
Camp Theme..................... ANABEL, MAX, OLIVER, STEWART
What's Your Deal?.....................CARMEN, OLIVER, STEWART
Hot Mess ....ANABEL
Who Do You Think I Am?...........ANABEL, CARMEN, MAX, STEWART
Labels.. OLIVER
Working Toward Tomorrow...................................ALL
Like, Whoa...ALL
Cinderella Song............................... OLIVER, STEWART
Shine .... CARMEN
Never Doubt My Love ....ALL
Take This Chance.................................... STEWART
Selfishly... MAX
Love Always, Me....................... ANABEL, OLIVER, STEWART
Life's Too Short/Open Your Heart ....ALL
Finale...ALL

ACT I

Scene One

(Exterior - Camp Entryway)

*(**ANABEL** and **OLIVER** enter, waving goodbye to unseen parents. Music starts under them – **"BEST SUMMER EVER."**)*

ANABEL & OLIVER. Byeeeeee!

ANABEL. I can't believe you stashed YOUR vodka in MY suitcase, of course Mom would find it!

OLIVER. Well at least she didn't find the joints I hid in your poncho.

ANABEL. What?! You did not!

(frantically searching through her bag)

Oliver, this is our job!

These kids are only 11 years old!

We're shaping young minds here!

OLIVER. You shape, I'll smoke.

(sings)

I'VE BEEN WAITING EIGHTEEN YEARS
TO FINALLY GET AWAY
AS THEY SAY, WHEN THE CAT'S AWAY
THE EAGER MICE WILL PLAY!
I'LL BE HERE FOR TWO WHOLE MONTHS
WITH MY PRE-PUBESCENT TWIN
FOR ME IT'S NOT ABOUT THE CAMPERS
MUCH TO HER CHAGRIN!
IT'LL BE THE BEST SUMMER EVER!
I'LL HAVE THE BEST SUMMER EVER!
HERE'S TO THE BEST SUMMER EVER
AND IT STARTS TODAY!

ANABEL. *(handing **OLIVER** the joints)* Here, take these, I'm not getting fired before we even start.

OLIVER. *(sarcastic)* Like you'd ever get fired; you're more wholesome than Hermione Granger.

ANABEL. Whatever, someone has to look out for your butt.

OLIVER. *(getting out iPhone)* Don't worry Anabel, I'll find someone to look out for my butt.

ANABEL. Are you on Craigslist again? Put that way!

   (sings)

   I CAN'T WAIT TO MEET MY CAMPERS
   JUST THINK THE THINGS WE'LL DO
   KEEPING JOURNALS, MAKING LANYARDS
   STAYING UP TIL TWO
   I'LL BE HERE FOR JUST TWO MONTHS
   AND I'M SURE THE TIME WILL FLY
   I'LL MAKE THE MOST OF EVERY MINUTE
   AT LEAST I'M GONNA TRY
   TO HAVE THE BEST SUMMER EVER
   I'LL HAVE THE BEST SUMMER EVER
   HERE'S TO THE BEST SUMMER EVER
   AND IT STARTS TODAY!

OLIVER. Apparently, there are only 2 gay men within a 5 mile radius, and they're both married. I guess I'll have to wait until New York!

ANABEL. I can't believe you're moving to New York after the summer, I will never go there – it's so dirty and you can never find a public bathroom!

   (STEWART *walks in.)*

OLIVER. Nevermind, crisis averted.

ANABEL. Who's that?

STEWART. *(to offstage)* Yes Dad, I'm fine! Just go!

   (sings)

   I CAN'T STAND THEIR CONSTANT BADGERING
   SO GLAD I'M OUT OF THERE
   I JUST NEED THE TIME TO BE

THE BOY WHO DOESN'T CARE
LETTING LOOSE FOR THESE TWO MONTHS
WITH NO FAMILY IN SIGHT
STANDING ON MY OWN FOR ONCE
I KNOW I'LL BE ALRIGHT
THIS IS THE BEST SUMMER EVER
I'LL HAVE THE BEST SUMMER EVER
HERE'S TO THE BEST SUMMER EVER
AND IT STARTS TODAY!

ALL 3.

OH YEAH
IT STARTS TODAY
I'M SURE THE TIME WILL FLY
I CAN'T WAIT TO MEET MY CAMPERS
JUST THINK THE FUN WE'LL HAVE
IT STARTS TODAY!

ANABEL. Hey, are you a counselor too?

OLIVER. *(sarcastic)* No, he just looks really mature for eleven.

STEWART. Ha ha. Hey, I'm Stewart. Do you guys know where we check in?

OLIVER. I can check you in, date of birth, sex? Can I interview you for my video blog? My last one got 5,000 views.

ANABEL. Oliver stop, we don't even know him! Yeah, we just got here too. Let me look, I printed out directions to the mess hall.

OLIVER. You go, Dora the Explorer.

ANABEL. Cut it out!

STEWART. Um...are you guys...together?

OLIVER. Uh, she's my sister! Can't you see the family resemblance?

> (**ANABEL** *and* **OLIVER** *stand back to back, posing.*)

STEWART. *(laughs)* Oh maybe...

> (**CARMEN** *enters, riled up on her cell phone.*)

Uh...is she one of us?

OLIVER. Haha, Anabel, I think I found your co-counselor!

CARMEN. *(sings)*

> WHAT THE HELL, MOM?
> I CAN'T BELIEVE YOU MADE ME COME HERE
> THERE'S NO MALL AND THERE'S NO STARBUCKS
> ALL I SEE ARE DEER
> YOU'RE INSANE, YOU KNOW THAT I HATE KIDS
> YOU KNOW I DO
> BUT FOR YOU, I'LL TRY
> THOUGH I WANT TO DIE
> MOM, PLEASE DON'T CRY!

Ugh!

(speaks)

All these fucking flies!

(Alternate: All these effing flies!)

(beat, sarcastic)

Hey, I'm Carmen. This is gonna be the best summer ever.

(sings)

> BEST SUMMER EVER
> IT STARTS TODAY
> I'M SURE THAT THE TIME WILL FLY
> I CAN'T WAIT TO MEET MY CAMPERS
> I DON'T WANT TO MEET MY CAMPERS
> IT STARTS TODAY
> IT STARTS TODAY

*(**MAX** enters, music slows.)*

MAX.

> AND THERE'S WHERE I KISSED
> THAT GIRL FROM BUNK FIVE
> THE ROAD WHERE I LEARNED TO DRIVE
> THE SMELL OF THE AIR
> THERE'S NO PLACE ELSE WHERE
> I FEEL LIKE I'M ALIVE
> I'M FEELING SO ALIVE
> HI I'M MAX

ANABEL. *(speaks)* Hi Max!

(sings)

I'M ANABEL, AND HERE'S MY BROTHER
IT'S OUR FIRST TIME HERE AT CAMP

MAX.

HA, I'VE BEEN COMING HERE FOR TEN YEARS

STEWART.

WHERE DO WE PUT OUR STUFF?

ANABEL.

DOES IT GET COLD AT NIGHT?

OLIVER.

AND WHAT ABOUT TV?

ANABEL. Oliver!

OLIVER.

I CAN'T LIVE WITHOUT MY BUFFY!

STEWART. Who watches Buffy?

MAX.

GUYS, RELAX
WHAT'S THE DEAL WITH THAT GIRL OVER THERE?

ANABEL.

HER NAME IS CARMEN

STEWART & OLIVER. She's busy…

STEWART.

ON THE PHONE

OLIVER. She's probably sexting.

ANABEL. You're so crass!

MAX.

IT'S ALRIGHT
SHE WILL COME AROUND, THERE'S TIME
BUT WE HAVE GOT SOME WORK TO DO
TO START
THE BEST SUMMER EVER

ALL 5.

> BEST SUMMER EVER
> IT STARTS TODAY
> I'M SURE THAT THE TIME WILL FLY
> I CAN'T WAIT TO MEET MY CAMPERS
> I DON'T WANT TO MEET MY CAMPERS
> IT STARTS
> IT STARTS
> IT STARTS
> IT STARTS...

LOUDSPEAKER. All campers please report to the mess hall for orientation!

ALL 5.

> TODAY!

(end of Scene One)

Scene Two

*(Lights up in the Mess Hall, the five counselors are seated on benches. MAX is standing, talking to the kids [the audience]. Underscored, "**CAMP THEME**" starts.)*

MAX. Now if this is your first summer here at camp, you may experience some things you've never seen before. This summer is all about fun, but with fun comes responsibility. Always remember to approach each new day with an open heart and an open mind and remember the number one tenet of Camp Timberlake, "live to love." Anabel, can you help me out with our Camp Timberlake song?

MAX & ANABEL. *(sing)*
LIVE TO LOVE
LOVE TO LIVE
LIFE'S TOO SHORT TO NOT FORGIVE
WITH NO REGRETS
LIVE FOR TODAY
JUST DAY BY DAY
(speaks)

MAX. Everyone!

(MAX and ANABEL are singing to the campers, STEWART and OLIVER are rolling their eyes but singing along, CARMEN is pointedly not singing.)

MAX, ANABEL, STEWART, OLIVER. *(singing)*
LIVE TO LOVE
LOVE TO LIVE
LIFE'S TOO SHORT TO NOT FORGIVE
WITH NO REGRETS
LIVE FOR TODAY
JUST DAY BY DAY

MAX. Break it down!

(MAX, OLIVER, ANABEL and STEWART dance and sing goofily.)

MAX, ANABEL, STEWART, OLIVER.
> LIVE TO LOVE
> LOVE TO LIVE
> LIFE'S TOO SHORT TO NOT FORGIVE
> WITH NO REGRETS
> LIVE FOR TODAY
> JUST DAY BY DAY

CARMEN. *(simultaneously)* This is so lame.

(song ends)

MAX. Ok guys, quiet coyote.

(MAX does "quiet coyote" hand gesture.)

Due to an unfortunate incident last summer involving Diet Coke, Mentos and bumper boats, you are all now required to pass a swim test! Everyone follow…

(looks around)

Carmen to the waterfront! Single file!

CARMEN. *(to OLIVER)* Where the hell's the waterfront? I am not getting my hair wet.

(looks at others, nobody is helping)

Guys, come on, someone help me. Seriously!

(beat, last resort)

Ugh! I've got some…

(mimes smoking a joint or cigarette)

…for later, if you help me!

(OLIVER and STEWART shrug.)

OLIVER. Alright, let's do it. Stewart?

STEWART. Ok everyone, follow Oliver and Carmen. You, with the headgear. Can that get wet?

CARMEN. Guys, these kids have rattails. Where are we?

STEWART. *(at back of line, to ANABEL)* Hey, are you coming?

(motions that they are going to smoke)

ANABEL. *(hesitant)* No, no, I have to finish laminating some name tags. I didn't know there were so many ways to spell "Christina."

STEWART. Ok. Well, I'll see ya later then.

> (OLIVER, CARMEN *and* STEWART *exit, leaving* MAX *and* ANABEL *onstage.* MAX *feels his phone ring, he takes it out.*)

MAX. Hey what's up? No...I'm not alone, is it serious? Oh... ok well I'll call you back in an hour.

> (MAX *hangs up his phone, as* ANABEL *comes over, oblivious.*)

ANABEL. Hey!

MAX. Hey!

ANABEL. You're so good with them, they love you.

MAX. The kids?

ANABEL. Yeah, I hope I can be a really great counselor like you someday.

MAX. Ah, well it's just takes practice, I've been doing this for a while. It's funny, they love it when you're corny. I remember my favorite counselor used to name us after candy and we ate it up. I was Big League Chew.

ANABEL. I wasn't allowed to eat Big League Chew, too much sugar. Also, it's like chewing tobacco. Grasty. That's a combination of nasty and gross...I made it up myself. Uh...I'm so weird.

> (*Awkward silence.* MAX *changes the subject.*)

MAX. Umm...have you seen the new arts and crafts studio? They bought like 500 new brushes.

ANABEL. How did the paintbrush die?

MAX. What?

ANABEL. It had a stroke!

MAX. (*inward groan*) Come on!

> (*They exit.*)

> (*end of Scene Two*)

> (*Lights down.*)

Scene Three

(Exterior - Field)

(**OLIVER**, **CARMEN** *and* **STEWART** *are seated on the bleachers, smoking.)*

OLIVER. That lifeguard can keep those kids all day for all I care.

STEWART. Yeah, as soon as Christina put the other Christina's knee scab in her mouth, I had to get out of there.

CARMEN. Ew. I didn't see that, I was busy listening to the Cohen twins argue about their bat mitzah theme. It came down to Jersey Shore versus Twilight.

STEWART. If Taylor Lautner shows up, I'm so there.

OLIVER. *(perks up)* Oh really?

STEWART. *(jokingly)* Although, Snooki's pretty hot too.

OLIVER. What?! Are you gay or not?

STEWART. Labels are for clothes. Sometimes I like Zac Efron, sometimes I'm more in the mood for some Miley. I'm really open to anything.

CARMEN. So you're just a slut?

STEWART. I prefer the term "pansexual."

CARMEN. So pretty much you'll sleep with anything.

STEWART. *(mocking)* No, it means I have an acute penchant for the Greek god Pan.

(long pause)

OLIVER. Like Pan's Labyrinth?

STEWART. *(sarcastic)* Basically I'll sleep with anything.

*(Piano starts – **"WHAT'S YOUR DEAL?"**)*

CARMEN. I call that a flaming hot mess.

OLIVER. *(sings)*
SO WHAT'S YOUR DEAL?
SAY IT'S TEN PM ON FRIDAY
ARE YOU OUT OR STAYING IN?
SO WHAT'S YOUR DEAL?

OLIVER. *(cont.)*

> DO YOU GO OUT TO THE MOVIES?
> OR DO YOU DVR INSTEAD?
> BOXERS OR BRIEFS, COFFEE OR TEA
> DO YOU LISTEN TO MARIAH?
> I'M A WHITNEY GUY MYSELF
> (CHIN VIBRATO!)
> SALTY OR SWEET, MAC OR PC?
> IT'S THE LITTLE THINGS THAT MATTER
> WE'LL BE SPENDING SO MUCH TIME TOGETHER
>
> SO WHAT'S YOUR DEAL?
> TELL ME ALL THERE IS TO KNOW
> DON'T HOLD BACK, I WANT THE DIRT
> SO WHAT'S YOUR DEAL?
> WHAT'S YOUR PLAN AFTER THE SUMMER?
> LET'S ME GUESS, IT'S MIT? HARVARD? CLOWN COLLEGE?

STEWART.

> I'LL TELL YOU WHAT YOU NEED TO KNOW
> I CAN'T REVEAL MY SECRETS
> DID MY PARENTS SEND YOU HERE?
> TOO MANY QUESTIONS, JUST RELAX
> CAN WE PLEASE ENJOY THE SUNSHINE?
> WE HAVE A LOT OF TIME
> FOR THAT.

OLIVER. You are so weird.

STEWART. What? It's our first day!

OLIVER. Whatever, pass the joint.

STEWART. *(sings)*

> SO WHAT'S YOUR DEAL?

OLIVER. *(coughs on joint)*

> WHAT'S MY DEAL?
> YOU DON'T GET TO ASK THE QUESTIONS

STEWART.

> FINE!
> ARE YOU ALWAYS THIS UPTIGHT?
>
> That was rhetorical.
>
> *(laughs)*

CARMEN.

>YOU GUYS ARE KILLING ME!
>LET'S BACK THIS UP A LITTLE BIT
>CAN I ASK YOU BOTH A QUESTION?
>THAT GUY, MAX, WHO "LIVES TO LOVE"
>WHAT'S HIS DEAL, HE'S SUCH A WEIRDO
>HE SHOULD HAVE COME ALONG

OLIVER.

>HE'S WITH MY SISTER

STEWART. Anabel, right?

OLIVER.

>YEAH, THEY'RE BORING

CARMEN. You guys suck!

>(**CARMEN** *gets up to leave.*)

OLIVER.

>YOU'VE GOT SOMETHING IN YOUR HAIR...

>(**OLIVER** *picks a feather out of* **STEWART**'s *hair, they kiss, but* **STEWART** *pushes him away.* **CARMEN** *exits.*)

OLIVER & STEWART.

>WHAT'S HIS DEAL
>WHAT DOES HE WANT?

STEWART.

>WHAT THE FUCK?
>I NEED A MINUTE

OLIVER.

>WHY'S HE SENDING ME MIXED SIGNALS?

STEWART.

>WHAT'S MY DEAL?

OLIVER.

>WHAT'S HIS DEAL?

STEWART & OLIVER.

>WHY CAN'T HE SEE?

STEWART.

>I JUST NEED TIME TO BE...

OLIVER.
WHAT'S HIS DEAL?
(end of Scene Three)

Scene Four

(Interior - bunk)

LOUDSPEAKER. Attention all campers: tonight's evening activities will consist of Wild West Lasso Contest, Make-Your-Own-Milkshake, and a screening of the film "The Silence of the Lambs."

(Lights up on **ANABEL**, *who is making posters on a craft table.* **MAX** *is writing in his journal.)*

ANABEL. So then water is literally pouring out of their noses, and I'm like "sinus irrigation win!" Neti-pots are amazing!

MAX. Please don't tell me you brought one?

ANABEL. Well you know, just in case one of my campers was congested.

MAX. Haha, you're ridiculous! You're such a mom. Let me guess, you carry a Tide-to-Go Stick, don't you?

ANABEL. Stewart has already spilled bug juice on himself three times, he really needs someone to look out for him. You're right, I AM such a mom. God I'm lame.

MAX. You always say that. How are you lame?

ANABEL. Um, how many people do you know who have a subscription to Cat Fancy?

MAX. A cat lady at seventeen?

ANABEL. Oliver says I came out of the womb covered in cat hair.

MAX. Oh. That's pretty lame, Anabel.

ANABEL. SEE! Everyone says that.

MAX. But you know what, you probably should just own it. People will respect you more if you don't apologize for yourself.

ANABEL. It's not that simple. I'm not like you.

MAX. You just have to trust people and not be so afraid.

ANABEL. *(not sold)* Ok...

MAX. Can I trust *you*?

ANABEL. Yeah, of course.

MAX. Can I tell you something I just found out? I'm freaking out a little.

(He whispers in her ear.)

ANABEL. Oh my Gosh, Max. That's...that's...wow. What are you going to do?

(MAX gestures, as if to say, "God, who knows.")

MAX. Please don't tell anyone, I just want to have a good drama-free summer.

(Heading out, he turns back.)

Hey. What does a cat call a bowl of mice?

ANABEL. What?

MAX. A purrrfect meal!

ANABEL. Now *that* is lame!

(MAX exits quickly. ANABEL sits pensively for a second.)

ANABEL. *(to herself)* A purrrfect meal! Hahaha!

(CARMEN, STEWART and OLIVER come in, laughing and joking around.)

STEWART. *(to ANABEL)* Hey, have you been here the whole time?

ANABEL. Yeah, I'm just working on these posters for the counselor play, Cinderella!

OLIVER. *(picks a poster up)* It looks like Michael's Crafts had a firesale on LAME GOODS.

(All laugh except ANABEL.)

STEWART. Hey we're gonna go play beer pong on the tennis courts. Oliver said he smuggled some 40s in his rain boots.

(OLIVER gets in ANABEL's face with his video camera.)

ANABEL. You don't have rain boots, get that away from me!

OLIVER. I meant your rain boots. Anabel, you'll never be an internet sensation like me with that attitude.

(**OLIVER** *grabs her rain boots and pulls a 40 oz. out of one.*)

CARMEN. Oh, those are really cute.

(**CARMEN** *takes the rain boots and exits.*)

STEWART. *(beat)* Well you should come! Oliver wants to film us lip-syncing to a Madonna music video.

OLIVER. *(interrupting, glaring at* **ANABEL***)* She's busy practicing being boring.

(**OLIVER** *makes large gesture behind* **STEWART***'s back to* **ANABEL***, indicating "he's mine!")*

ANABEL. *(pauses)* …I think I'm just gonna finish these. Maybe I'll see you guys at the movie?

OLIVER. Ok, bye…

(**OLIVER** *exits.*)

STEWART. Are you sure?

ANABEL. *(clearly conflicted)* Yeah, I probably shouldn't.

(half smiles)

STEWART. Ok, well if you change your mind, I've got a Colt 45 with your name on it.

(**STEWART** *exits.*)

ANABEL. I don't know what that is…

(Music starts – "HOT MESS")

(sings)

PRIM AND PROPER, ANNOYING
TRIM AND TIDY, AND CLOYING
JUST NAME YOUR SUBJECT AND I'LL PROVIDE
A VISITOR'S GUIDE

PRUDE AND PRACTICALLY BLINDED
SHREWD AND TACTICALLY-MINDED
I THINK MY DISPOSITION PUTS ME
IN THIS POSITION, AND

ANABEL. *(cont.)*

I FEEL THIS UTTER FRUSTRATION
A KIND OF HUMILIATION
IT CUTS ME TO THE BONE
WHEN THE CHEESE STANDS ALONE!

CAUSE I FEEL LIKE A
HOT MESS, I'M TIED UP IN
KNOTS, YES!
THIS ISN'T THE LIFE
THAT I WANT FOR ME
SO JUST WAIT AND SEE
I'LL PUT ON SOME
FISHNETS, AND SHOW OFF MY
ASSETS
SMOKE CIGARETTES!
BUT FOR NOW, I GUESS
I'M JUST A HOT MESS
LOOK AT ME, GOD BLESS
I'M SUCH A HOT MESS

I'M A HOT MESS!

ALWAYS THE ONLY ONE SOBER
WITH CHRISTMAS LIGHTS IN OCTOBER
I'M LAME AND YOU CAN BANK IT
I'M YOUR OWN BIG WET BLANKET!

I FEEL THIS UTTER FRUSTRATION
A KIND OF HUMILIATION
MY NOSE COULDN'T BE ANY BROWNER
AND I'M SUCH A DEBBIE DOWNER!

CAUSE I FEEL LIKE A
HOT MESS, I'M TIED UP IN
KNOTS, YES!
THIS ISN'T THE LIFE
THAT I WANT FOR ME
SO JUST WAIT AND SEE
I COULD PUT ON SOME
HOT PANTS, TAKE SHOTS AND
FREAK DANCE

ANABEL. *(cont.)*

> HAVE A STEAMY ROMANCE
> BUT FOR NOW, I GUESS
> I'M JUST A HOT MESS
> LOOK AT ME, GOD BLESS
> I'M SUCH A HOT MESS
>
> WHAT DO I SAY
> THAT PUSHES THEM SO FAR AWAY?
> WHY DO I FEEL THIS WAY?
>
> I GUESS, I CONFESS I GOT STRESS
> UNDUE DURESS, ALL FROM THIS MESS
> I WON'T SUPPRESS MY SUCCESS,
> I JUST WON'T BE A
>
> HOT MESS, I'M TIED UP IN
> KNOTS, YES!
> THIS ISN'T THE LIFE
> THAT I WANT FOR ME
> SO JUST WAIT AND SEE
> I'LL BE A HOT SLUT, MAKE OUT AND
> READ SMUT
> I'LL BE A HOT SHOT, GET DRUNK AND
> SMOKE POT
> GO ON A HOT DATE, FLIRT, KISS AND
> GYRATE!
> (EEK!)
>
> THEY'RE ON LIFE'S ROLLER COASTER
> WHILE I'M FINISHING A POSTER
>
> (Look I made a poster!)
>
> THOUGH I MIGHT OBSESS
> I KNOW I'LL DIE UNLESS
> I PUT OUT THIS HOT FLAMING
>
> (**ANABEL** *rips up the poster.*)
>
> MESS!
> *(spoken)* Where's the tape!?

(end of Scene Four)

Scene Five

(Interior - bunk)

(CARMEN is on the phone with her mom.)

CARMEN. Mom, we talk about this everyday!

(ANABEL comes in.)

It's nobody's fault. You aren't the only one hurting here.

(sees ANABEL)

I have to go, my friend is here. I love you.

(CARMEN hangs up the phone.)

ANABEL. Hey, sorry, am I interrupting something?

CARMEN. Oh, no, my Mom's being crazy.

ANABEL. You talk to her a lot. I talk to my mom a lot, but mostly about fabric swatches. She's been redoing the living room for 10 years.

CARMEN. *(sniffs disgustedly)* You smell like bleach. Where were you?

ANABEL. I ran into Stewart on bathroom duty. He was trying to clean the toilet with hand sanitizer.

CARMEN. *(incredulous)* You just "ran into" Stewart in the boy's bathroom?

ANABEL. Oh…yeah, it was so random…

CARMEN. You like him, don't you?

ANABEL. *(flustered)* What? Stewart? No, we're just friends!

CARMEN. *(needling)* Shut up, don't play dumb with me, you like him! You turn bright red whenever he's in the room.

ANABEL. No, I don't!

(beat)

You can't tell anyone! Can this be our secret?

CARMEN. Fine, fine, but you should go for him.

ANABEL. Eh, we'll see. I'm not really like that. Now YOU tell me a secret.

CARMEN. Like what? I, uh…sometimes wear a Bumpit in my hair.

ANABEL. That's not a secret! Tell me a real one!

CARMEN. You know how I made fun of your clarinet? I used to play the flute.

ANABEL. Ok, well I still need something juicier, like, why are you always on the phone with your mom?

CARMEN. *(pauses…thinking if she'll reveal or not)* My brother died 3 months ago.

ANABEL. Oh…wow…I'm SO sorry. Do you want to talk about it?

CARMEN. Not really. It's been a rough few months.

(beat)

Everyone thinks that I'm a raging bitch, but I don't know how else to be right now.

ANABEL. I had no idea.

(beat)

I just watched a talk show on… grieving… and you just have to give it time, Carmen.

CARMEN. I know, that's what everyone says, but that doesn't make it any easier.

(sighs)

You and your talk shows.

(half smiles)

I actually think I saw that one too,

ANABEL & CARMEN. *(slowly starting, then getting louder)* Dateline Special Report with Ann Curry and Stone Phillips?

CARMEN. Shut up, get out of my brain.

ANABEL. Can I ask you something?

CARMEN. No.

ANABEL. *(taking her seriously)* Uh..er…um…

CARMEN. I'm just kidding, what is it?!

ANABEL. It's about Stewart. Do you really think he would like me? Can you kind of secretly ask him, but don't let him know that I like him?

CARMEN. What is this, high school?

(ANABEL *makes a face indicating "uh, yeah!"*)

No, you ask him.

ANABEL. *(whiny)* But I'm not like that!

CARMEN. You know what, this is what we'll do. I want to talk to Max, and you need to talk to Stewart. Let's switch our rounds tonight. That way, we'll each get some alone time.

ANABEL. Won't we get in trouble?

CARMEN. Shut up, who cares, we're in charge, remember?

ANABEL. Haha ok.

(*beat, looks at* CARMEN*'s phone*)

Oh shoot what time is it? Riflery just ended! I have to pick up my kids!

CARMEN. Hey wait…thanks for talking to me. That was the first real conversation I've had this summer.

ANABEL. Of course.

(CARMEN *and* ANABEL *hug.*)

LOUDSPEAKER. Attention: could the counselor for Bunk 9 please pick up their campers at Riflery? It's about to get "Lord of the Flies" up in here.

ANABEL. Ah! Thanks loudspeaker!

(ANABEL *exits quickly.*)

(*Lights down.*)

(*end of Scene Five*)

Scene Six

(Exterior - Spilt Stage: rounds)

*(**MAX** is seated in a lawnchair. **CARMEN** enters, silently. Music starts: "**WHO DO YOU THINK I AM?**")*

MAX. Hey, I said lights out! I'm talking to you, Bunk 5!

CARMEN. Look at you, such a hard-ass.

MAX. Haha shut up, yesterday they stayed up all night and Christina fell asleep during arts and crafts. Another kid glued her hair to the table.

CARMEN. You live you learn.

(sings)

HAS ANYONE TOLD YOU
YOU'D MAKE A GOOD FARMER?

MAX. What?!

CARMEN.

I MEAN YOU'VE GOT
THE PERFECT TAN

MAX. Shut up, what are you doing here? Where's Anabel?

CARMEN.

I ASKED TO SWITCH
I WANTED TO SEE YOU

MAX. Well, here I am.

JUST ANOTHER NIGHT OF ROUNDS

CARMEN.

AREN'T YOU GETTING COLD IN THAT T-SHIRT?

MAX.

I DON'T FEEL A CHILL, BUT THANKS

CARMEN.

WATCH WHERE YOU GO POINTING YOUR FLASHLIGHT

MAX.

WHO DO YOU THINK I AM?

*(**STEWART** is sitting in a lawn chair on the opposite side of the stage. **ANABEL** enters.)*

STEWART.

AREN'T YOU SUPPOSED TO BE OUT WITH MAX?

Whatever, come sit down.

CAN I BORROW SOME BUGSPRAY?

MY LEGS...ITCH

ANABEL. Oh! Hold on one second! Let me find...oh!

HERE YOU GO

LOOK IT'S SPF 45!

STEWART.

YOU'RE AWARE THAT IT'S DARK OUT...RIGHT?

ANABEL.

SORRY

I GET SO AWKWARD SOMETIMES

STEWART.

STOP IT

IT'S JUST ME AND MY FLASHLIGHT

ANABEL.

SOMETIMES COUNTING STARS IS FUN...

(embarassed, shaking her head)

STEWART.

WE COULD HAVE MORE FUN TOGETHER?

ANABEL.

WHO DO YOU THINK I AM?

(Back to **MAX** *and* **CARMEN**, *both sides are lit now.)*

CARMEN.

YOU'VE BEEN WEIRD

THIS WHOLE WEEK

CAN'T YOU SEE

I'M INTERESTED?

MAX.

I'M JUST BUSY

WATCHING THE KIDS

YOU DON'T WANT TO KNOW

ABOUT ME

STEWART.
> YOU HAVE GOT SUCH
> PRETTY HAIR
> WHY DO YOU WEAR IT
> UP LIKE THAT?

ANABEL.
> KATHIE LEE SAYS
> WASH AND GO!
> SHOULD I TAKE IT DOWN?

CARMEN.
> WHAT ARE YOU TALKING ABOUT?
> I HOOFED IT THROUGH THE WOODS
> AT MIDNIGHT TO SEE YOU!

MAX.
> DON'T YOU THINK I SEE THROUGH YOUR TRICKS?
> I KNOW ALL ABOUT THESE GAMES THAT YOU'RE PLAYING
> PLEASE JUST SHOW ME THE GIRL INSIDE
> YOU CAN'T FOOL ME
> WHO DO YOU THINK I AM?

ANABEL.
> THIS IS GOING BETTER THAN PLANNED

STEWART.
> GIVE ME A CHANCE, YOU WON'T REGRET IT

ANABEL.
> TELL ME MORE ABOUT THAT KID WHO EATS CRAYONS

STEWART. Hey! I'm a good counselor!
> WHO DO YOU THINK I AM?

ALL 4.
> HOW CAN I?
> HOW CAN I?
> HOW CAN I?

ANABEL. Hey, get back in your bunk! Go back to sleep…or else! Yeah…

STEWART. Go Anabel! You TELL that raccoon!

ANABEL. Shut up! Raccoons need their sleep too!

> (**ANABEL** *and* **STEWART** *are cuddling in their lawn-chairs. They don't kiss.*)

CARMEN.

YOU MAKE ME FEEL KINDA CRAZY

YOU'RE DIFFERENT FROM MOST OTHER GUYS

MAX.

SO LET'S BE DIFFERENT TOGETHER

MAX & CARMEN.

AND YOU'LL SEE WHO I AM

(**MAX** *and* **CARMEN** *share an innocent kiss. Lights down.*)

(*end of Scene Six*)

Scene Seven

(Lights up on **OLIVER** *and* **CARMEN** *in the boys' bunk, playing truth or dare.)*

CARMEN. Ok, truth or dare.

OLIVER. Truth.

CARMEN. So. What's going on with you and Stewart? You might have to fight Anabel for him.

OLIVER. *(laughing)* Anabel is gonna have 40 cats and a prison penpal; I'm really not worried about her in competition with me.

CARMEN. Well you should watch out, you never know!

OLIVER. Well whatever, I'm pushing and pushing for Stewart, but he's giving me mixed signals. He's so hard to read.

CARMEN. *(laughs)* Good luck with that.

OLIVER. *(sassily)* I always get my man. Truth or dare.

CARMEN. Dare.

OLIVER. I dare you…to take a bra photo on your phone and send it to Max.

CARMEN. Ew, no.

OLIVER. Whatever, prude. I'll take a dare.

CARMEN. Ok…Stewart left his computer open again. I dare you to look in his inbox.

*(***OLIVER** *goes over to* **STEWART***'s laptop.)*

OLIVER. Oo, playing dirty now! I don't know his password.

CARMEN. Please,

(sings "Party in the USA" melody)

"party-in-the-stew-s-a."

OLIVER. Ah! Haha! Ok. I'm in. Let's see. First…from: Amazon.com, confirmation of purchase. Yanni: Live at the Acropolis.

(They look at each other and roll their eyes.)

CARMEN. Oh geez. Ok, what else?

OLIVER. Oh, this one's from his Mom. Hi Stewey-pooey…

CARMEN. HA!

OLIVER. …I just wanted to let you know that I e-mailed Dartmouth, and I gave them a heads up that you wanted to live in the all-boys substance free dorm. Love always, Mom.

CARMEN. He's going to Dartmouth?!

OLIVER. Why wouldn't he just tell us that!?

CARMEN. Weird.

OLIVER. Ok, truth or dare.

CARMEN. Oh I actually have to run, that reminded me that I have to go call my mom about MY dorm assignment.

OLIVER. Wow, Anabel got recruited by Notre Dame, Stewart's going to Dartmouth, and you're smart too. Kill me now.

CARMEN. Whatever, let it all out in your video blog. I'll see you later.

(**CARMEN** exits. **OLIVER** sets up tripod and flipcam.)

OLIVER. Hey guys, I know I haven't updated in a while, but I've been kinda busy out in the middle of nowhere.

(Music starts – "LABELS.")

Anyway, let's get down to business. Today's video blog is all about labels. Let me start with a story.

(sings)

I'M IN LINE WITH MY CHOCOLATE MILK AND FRIES
RIGHT BEHIND THIS PACK OF SOCCER GUYS
THEY HAVE THE MOST AMAZING THIGHS
(THOSE SOCCER GUYS)

ANYWAY, I PAY AND GRAB MY TRAY
I GO TO SIT WITH MY BEST FRIEND RENEE
BUT SOCCER GUYS, TO MY SURPRISE

THEY'VE TAKEN MY SEAT AT THE POPULAR TABLE
RENDERING ME COMPLETELY UNABLE
TO HOLD MY COURT IN THE CAFETORIUM
I LOOK AND I LOOK, THERE'S ONLY ONE SEAT

OLIVER. *(cont.)*

> BESIDE THAT KID WHO SMELLS LIKE STREET MEAT
> IT'S SOCIAL SUICIDE
> TO SIT RIGHT BY HIS SIDE

(speaks)

But then I thought to myself, Oliver...

(sings)

> THE MINUTE THAT YOU DO
> YOU MIGHT CHANGE YOUR POINT OF VIEW
> TAKE ALL YOU THOUGHT WAS TRUE
> AND THROW IT AWAY
> I GAVE THE KID A SHOT
> AND IN TURN I LEARNED A LOT
> THAT LABELS AREN'T FOR PEOPLE
> THEY'RE FOR CLOTHES

(speaks)

Alright, now it's time to read the "Dear Oliver" love letter of the week. This one's from Steven in New Jersey.

(sings)

> DEAR OLIVER, CAN YOU HELP ME OUT
> I'VE GOT A CRUSH ON A FELLOW EAGLE SCOUT
> *(aside)* THOSE EARTHY EAGLE SCOUTS
> THEY WEIRD ME OUT

> ANYWAY, YOU SEE MY PROBLEM HERE
> I'VE NEVER THOUGHT THAT I WOULD BE A QUEER
> BUT I LIKE GUYS, SO PLEASE ADVISE

> I LOVE THE WAY THAT HE STARTS A FIRE
> BLOWING THE FLAMES TO MAKE THEM GO HIGHER
> ANYTHING IT TAKES TO EARN THAT BADGE
> *(spoken)* Weird.

> I DON'T KNOW WHAT IT IS THAT I'M FEELING
> CAN'T BELIEVE IT, MY HEAD IS REELING
> TELL ME NOW, WHAT DO I DO?

OLIVER. *(cont.)*

YOURS TRULY
STEVEN
DEAR STEVEN

(clears throat)

Ahem.

COME OUT.

CAUSE THE MINUTE THAT YOU DO
YOU MIGHT CHANGE YOUR POINT OF VIEW
TAKE ALL YOU THOUGHT WAS TRUE
AND THROW IT AWAY
JUST GIVE THE KID A SHOT
AND IN TURN YOU'LL LEARN A LOT
THAT LABELS AREN'T FOR PEOPLE

THEY'RE FOR CARS
LAMBOURGHINI, BENTLEY, SAAB, ASTIN MARTIN
CADILLAC AND BMW
THEY'RE FOR SHOES
JIMMY CHOO, GUCCI, PRADA, COLE HAAN
CHRISTIAN LOUBOUTIN AND TORY BURCH
THEY'RE FOR JEANS
TRUE RELIGION, SEVENS, PAPER DENIM CLOTH, DIESEL
JOE'S, ROCK AND REPUBLIC
AND THEY'RE FOR CRAP
THE GAP, OLD NAVY, AND FOREVER 21

BUT ALL THOSE THINGS ARE SIMPLY ON THE SURFACE
TO JUDGE WOULD BE UNFAIR
SO DON'T YOU DARE DO YOURSELF A DISSERVICE
TAKE YOUR LABELS AND LEAVE THEM ALL BEHIND

CAUSE THE MINUTE THAT YOU DO
YOU MIGHT CHANGE YOUR POINT OF VIEW
TAKE ALL YOU THOUGHT WAS TRUE
AND THROW IT ALL AWAY
JUST GIVE IT ALL A SHOT
AND IN TURN YOU'LL LEARN A LOT

OLIVER. *(cont.)*
>THAT LABELS AREN'T FOR PEOPLE
>THAT LABELS AREN'T FOR PEOPLE
>THAT LABELS AREN'T FOR PEOPLE
>THEY'RE FOR CLOTHES
>
>*(speaks)*
>
>And recording artists, wink wink!
>
>*(Lights down.)*
>
>*(end of Scene Seven)*

Scene Eight

(ANABEL and CARMEN are walking together across the stage. Underscore: "What's Your Deal?" theme.)

ANABEL. So you kissed him?! What was it like?! Tell me all the details.

CARMEN. Whoa, down girl, it was just a kiss. It was good though.

ANABEL. Did he like, put his tongue on your tongue?

CARMEN. *(shaking head)* Actually, he kind of tasted like candy.

ANABEL. *(to herself)* Big League Chew!

CARMEN. What?

ANABEL. Oh, nevermind. So everything's OK between you two? He's told you everything?

CARMEN. Everything what?

ANABEL. Oh nevermind.

CARMEN. You're so weird. Come on!

(CARMEN beckons ANABEL offstage.)

(end of Scene Eight)

Scene Nine

(Lights up on the lounge, **OLIVER.** *and* **STEWART** *are watching the kids, at the pool, with whistles.)*

STEWART. Ok, you can go in, but no splashing this time!

*(***STEWART*** blows his whistle.)*

OLIVER. Wait, so you're saying that under no circumstance is it okay to pay for sex?

STEWART. Well yeah, it's more complicated than you might think. Not every prostitute does it because they want to – women are trafficked for sex every day only because there's demand for it.

OLIVER. *(dubious)* And you think stricter regulation would stop the trafficking?

STEWART. Well it's clearly not that easy, but supporting the industry in any way makes you complicit in the larger problem.

OLIVER. But...

(beat)

You're really smart.

STEWART. *(embarrassed)* Shut up.

OLIVER. No really, you are!

STEWART. I'm book smart. Not real smart.

(to unseen camper)

Hey, no diving in the shallow end!

OLIVER. Well "book smart" got you into Dartmouth, Stewey-pooey!

STEWART. How do you know about Dartmouth?

OLIVER. Doesn't matter. That's a great school though.

STEWART. Yeah whatever. Another thing my parents can brag about at the country club. I don't even want to go.

OLIVER. Dartmouth is in the middle of nowhere, isn't it?

STEWART. Exactly. It clearly wasn't my first choice, but my dad would only pay for Dartmouth. He's a legacy; I was conceived in his fraternity basement.

OLIVER. Ew. But YOU'RE the one who is going to have to spend 4 years there, not your father. So you should go where you want.

STEWART. They refuse to pay for any other school, so I kind of don't have any other choice.

OLIVER. You always have a choice. If I did everything my parents wanted, I'd be straight and next in line to take over the family hardware store. But I'm moving to New York!

STEWART. What are you gonna do in New York?

OLIVER. I don't know, I'll figure it out though.

STEWART. You really don't have a plan?

OLIVER. You don't need a plan, you just need a goal and a little confidence. What's the worst thing that would happen if you didn't go to Dartmouth?

STEWART. My parents would probably disown me. You don't get it, they've had my life mapped out since I was in the womb. They see me as an investment.

OLIVER. Listen, Stewart, obviously I really like you, but I'm gonna be honest, you have to do what's going to make YOU happy.

STEWART. I don't even know what would make ME happy.

OLIVER. Well that's what you need to figure out. At the end of the day, it's YOUR life, not theirs.

LOUDSPEAKER. Attention: Will Oliver from Bunk 4 please report to the main office? You have a special package waiting for you.

STEWART. I know ONE thing: I don't want to go to Dartmouth...but beyond that, I don't know.

(beat, joking)

Does that loudspeaker sound kind of gay to you?

OLIVER. *(evading the question)* Oh I never thought about it. Look Stewart, I'm always here if you want to talk more about it. I really think you should do what makes YOU happy.

STEWART. Ok…

(**OLIVER** *starts to exit, but comes back and hugs* **STEWART.**)

OLIVER. It'll all be ok. I promise.

(**OLIVER** *exits.*)

STEWART. *(to unseen camper)* Hey, will you please stop humping the pool noodle?

(end of Scene Nine)

Scene Ten

(Lights up on the dock. **MAX** *is sitting, pensive with notebook.* **CARMEN** *sneaks up behind him.)*

CARMEN. Hey, I've been looking for you. What are you doing out here by yourself?

MAX. Oh, nothing really…just writing.

CARMEN. *(teasing)* Playing with your flashlight?

MAX. Shut up! Hey, listen to this:

Doubt thou the stars are fire,

Doubt thou the sun doth move,

Doubt truth to be a liar,

But never doubt I love.

Isn't that beautiful?

CARMEN. That's *Hamlet* right? We read that last year.

(pause)

See that constellation up there?

MAX. Which one?

*(***CARMEN*** points at the sky.)*

CARMEN. The Seven Sisters. There are seven stars, but sometimes you can only see six. Sometimes the seventh one doesn't shine. My mom used to tell me whenever I was upset, that that was my star, and when it wasn't shining, she knew I was sad.

MAX. Maybe it *is* always shining, but sometimes, you just can't see it.

(beat)

CARMEN. I can't believe we've only been here a month. I feel like I know you so well.

MAX. Well we HAVE spent every night together for the past 3 weeks.

CARMEN. *(jokingly)* Whatever, you love it, who else would play Battleship with you every night?

MAX. Battleship is better than your game of choice, Mall Madness.

(**CARMEN** *rumples up* **MAX**'s *hair playfully. Music starts – "WORKING TOWARD TOMORROW."*)

You know, I can't believe it took you a month to get your hair wet.

CARMEN. Haha the lake's dirty!

MAX. (*rolls eyes, beat*) Well are you glad you're here now?

CARMEN. It just took some adjustments. I'm not used to this...lifestyle. All this Kum-ba-ya, live to love stuff.

(*laughs*)

MAX. Well, it's not so bad. Come here, I'm cold.

(**MAX** *grabs* **CARMEN** *and they get closer.*)

CARMEN. (*sings*)
FOUR WEEKS AGO
I STEPPED OFF THAT SCHOOL BUS
CURSING MY MOTHER
FOR SENDING ME HERE
LOOKING AROUND
AT THE INNOCENT FACES
I DON'T BELONG
THIS MUCH IS CLEAR

EACH DAY I WAKE
LOOK AT MY SCHEDULE
TIME FOR BREAKFAST
PASTE ON A SMILE

AND I DON'T KNOW HOW TO DO THIS
I'M STUCK AS THE GIRL WHO'S SCARED TO MOVE ON
AND I TRY TO BE FEARLESS
IT'S TIME FOR ME TO LIVE
MY LIFE

FOUR WEEKS PASS BY
I'VE SLEPT, LIKE, THREE HOURS
FIVE HUNDRED PEOPLE
WITH TWO DOZEN SHOWERS
BUT I'M STILL THE ONE
WITH HER HEAD IN THE PAST

MAX *(simul.)*

 FOUR WEEKS PASS BY
 HOW DID WE COME TO THIS?
 JUST ONE KISS

CARMEN & MAX.

 I DON'T BELONG
 HOW LONG WILL THIS LAST

 AND I DON'T KNOW HOW TO DO THIS
 I'M (SHE'S) STUCK AS THE GIRL
 WHO'S SCARED TO LET GO
 AND I TRY TO BE FEARLESS
 IT'S TIME FOR ME TO LIVE
 MY LIFE

CARMEN.

 YOU'RE SO COOL
 COLLECTED AND CHARMING
 ALWAYS IN CONTROL
 OF YOUR LIFE
 I FIND YOU SO DISARMING

 I CAN BE SUCH A MESS

MAX.

 I CAN BE SUCH A MESS

CARMEN.

 CLOSED OFF AND COLD, I CONFESS

MAX.

 CLOSED OFF AND COLD, I CONFESS

 *(**ANABEL** enters.)*

CARMEN, MAX, & ANABEL.

 GIVE ME A CHANCE
 I'M READY
 I'M READY

CARMEN.

 I'M READY!

 *(Music stops, **MAX** kisses **CARMEN**. Music swells again, **OLIVER** and **STEWART** enter.)*

ANABEL, STEWART, & OLIVER.
> AND I DON'T KNOW HOW TO DO THIS
> I'M READY TO LEARN
> WATCH AND YOU'LL SEE
> THAT I'M WORKING TOWARD TOMORROW

ALL 5.
> I'M READY TO GIVE
> I'M READY TO LEARN
> I'M READY TO LIVE
> MY LIFE!

> *(Music swells, ends.* **MAX** *and* **CARMEN** *are kissing.)*

> *(lights down)*

> *(end of Scene Ten)*

> *(Playoff music: "Working Toward Tomorrow")*

Scene Eleven

(**ANABEL, OLIVER** *and* **STEWART** *are roasting marsh-mallows around the campfire.*)

ANABEL. Oliver, you're not properly roasting your marsh-mallow, it's only brown on one side.

OLIVER. You roast your way, and I'll roast mine. I happen to like it this way.

ANABEL. That really stresses me out.

STEWART. Anabel, I think you need a sip of this, it'll take the edge off.

(**STEWART** *motions a beer towards her.*)

OLIVER. She'll never drink it.

ANABEL. Actually…I think I will.

(**STEWART** *motions the beer again, she holds her hand out, like "wait."*)

OLIVER. Oh wait for it, she has to take out her Invisalign.

ANABEL. You'll be sorry when you have crooked teeth, and I –

(**ANABEL** *takes out her Invisalign/retainer and sucks in the saliva.*)

am in perfect orthodontial health.

STEWART. *(reflexively)* Orthodontic.

ANABEL. *(quickly)* What?

STEWART. Here, just drink this.

(**ANABEL** *nervously takes the beer in hand.*)

STEWART. I promise it doesn't taste that bad.

OLIVER. *(quickly)* That's what she said.

(**ANABEL** *takes a sip of beer.*)

ANABEL. Whoa.

(**ANABEL** *takes a bigger sip. She burps. Music starts:* **"LIKE, WHOA"**)

ANABEL. *(cont.)* *(sings)*

    MAYBE IT'S THE BEER
    OR MAYBE I'M NOT THINKING CLEARLY
    LOOK AT ME RIGHT HERE
    I'M BREAKING RULES, A NEW FRONTIER

    AND THIS IS THE MOST OUTLANDISH THING
    I'VE EVER DONE
    AND THIS MAY BE WRONG, I KNOW,
    BUT I THINK IT'S KINDA FUN

    THIS FEELING…WOW!
    JUST PINCH ME NOW!

    CAUSE I'M LIKE, WHOA
    BUT I'M LIKE, WHOA
    JUST GO WITH THE FLOW
    WHOA
    WHOA
    JUST GOING WITH THE FLOW

STEWART & OLIVER.

    (STEWART *looking at* **ANABEL,** **OLIVER** *lookig at* **STEWART** *)*

    MAYBE IT'S THE FIRE
    I FEEL THIS KIND OF MAD DESIRE
    I'M STRUNG OUT ON A WIRE
    GOD ONLY KNOWS WHAT WILL TRANSPIRE

    AND I WANT TO SHOUT IT OUT
    AT THE TOP OF MY LUNGS
    SOON WE'LL BE SWAPPING SPIT
    AND INTERTWINING TONGUES

ANABEL.

    THIS FEELING, WOW!

STEWART & OLIVER.

    THIS FEELING

ALL 3.

    JUST PINCH ME NOW!
    CAUSE I'M LIKE, WHOA
    BUT I'M LIKE, WHOA

ALL 3. *(cont.)*

 JUST GO WITH THE FLOW
 WHOA
 WHOA
 JUST GOING WITH THE FLOW
 CAUSE I'M LIKE, WHOA
 BUT I'M LIKE, WHOA
 JUST GO WITH THE FLOW
 WHOA
 WHOA
 JUST GOING WITH THE FLOW

 *(**MAX** and **CARMEN** come into view, holding hands.)*

CARMEN.

 YOU KINDA KISS LIKE A GIRL

MAX.

 YOU KINDA ACT LIKE A BOY

CARMEN.

 WHEN YOU DID THAT LITTLE TWIRL

MAX.

 YOU'RE JUST TRYING TO BE COY

CARMEN.

 CAN YOU FEEL THE SUMMER AIR?

MAX.

 I FEEL THE BUGS EVERYWHERE

CARMEN. *(points to a spot on her neck)*

 JUST SHUT UP AND KISS ME THERE

MAX.

 KISS YOU WHERE?

CARMEN.

 THERE!

 (They kiss playfully and enter the campfire zone.)

STEWART & OLIVER.

 I'M GONNA MAKE MY MOVE
 BEFORE THE NIGHT IS DONE

ALL 5.

 THIS MAY BE WRONG, I KNOW
 BUT I THINK IT'S KINDA FUN

ANABEL & CARMEN.
> THIS FEELING, WOW!

BOYS.
> THIS FEELING

ALL 5.
> JUST PINCH ME NOW!

OLIVER.
> IT'S TIME TO MAKE MY MOVE

ANABEL, STEWART, CARMEN, MAX.
> WHOA

OLIVER.
> I'M FEELING THE GROOVE

ANABEL, STEWART, CARMEN, MAX.
> WHOA

OLIVER.
> STEWART, HONEY, YOU'VE
> GOTTA UP THE FLIRTING
> CAUSE, BABY, I'M ASSERTING THAT
> WE'VE
> GOTTA DO IT THIS EVENING
> YOU GOTTA BELIEVE
> THIS FEVER JUST WON'T LEAVE, SO –

> (**ANABEL & STEWART** *get caught up in the moment and kiss, not realizing* **OLIVER** *sees them.*)

> Whoa...

> (**OLIVER** *backs out, shocked and angry.*)

ANABEL, STEWART, CARMEN, MAX.
> CAUSE I'M LIKE, WHOA
> BUT I'M LIKE, WHOA
> JUST GO WITH THE FLOW
> WHOA
> WHOA
> JUST GOING WITH THE FLOW

> CAUSE I'M LIKE, WHOA
> BUT I'M LIKE, WHOA

JUST GO WITH THE FLOW
WHOA
WHOA
JUST GOING WITH THE FLOW

ANABEL, STEWART, CARMEN, MAX. *(cont.)*

WHOA
WHOA
THIS FEELING IS LIKE
WHOA

(End of Scene Eleven)

Scene Twelve

(Auditorium)

*(Stage is split between "onstage" and "backstage." Backstage, **ANABEL**, **CARMEN**, **STEWART** and **MAX** are getting ready for the Cinderella show. Putting on makeup and handmade costumes, etc.)*

LOUDSPEAKER. Attention campers: please make your way to the auditorium for the annual counselor play "Cinderella." I love a good catfight, and it looks like this rags to riches tale *might* just get a little more rich.

ANABEL. Guys, oh my God! I think I saw the loudspeaker voice in person.

CARMEN. No way!

ANABEL. I was getting my kids from their miming workshop, and I heard someone practicing the oboe in the theater, and it was this guy I'd never seen before.

MAX. The loudspeaker plays the oboe?

STEWART. Are you surprised?

ANABEL. Well he needs to practice more, it sounded like a dying cat.

*(**OLIVER** enters, pissy.)*

Oh! Oliver, did you bring your body glitter that I asked to borrow?

OLIVER. *(curtly)* No.

ANABEL. …Oh, didn't you see the note I left?

OLIVER. *(nasty)* Here's a note: keep your hands to yourself.

STEWART. What's wrong with you?

MAX. Guys, it's places, let's go.

*(**MAX** and **STEWART** enter the stage area. The others are still getting ready.)*

MAX. *(narrating)* The next day, the prince set out to find Cinderella, the fair maiden whose pure and innocent heart enraptured his at the ball. All he had to aid his search was a dainty glass slipper Cinderella had dropped in her hasty exit.

(backstage)

OLIVER. You know I saw that last night.

ANABEL. Saw what?

OLIVER. I'm not stupid, Anabel.

(onstage)

(STEWART *enters, carrying a large cumbersome rain boot.)*

STEWART. Oh woe is me!

I have tried this glass slipper on every fragile female foot in this vast village, in a desperate attempt to find the beguiling beauty with whom I will explore this magnificent world. BUT! I have not lost hope! Onward ho!

(backstage)

OLIVER. *(accusatory)* You kissed Stewart. Right in front of me.

ANABEL. *(giddy)* I know, I was a little drunk!

OLIVER. Don't you get it? I *like* him.

(sarcastic)

Anabel wins again. I thought we looked out for each other, You know, you've really changed a lot.

(onstage)

MAX. The prince searched and searched and finally came upon a small house in the Catskills. *(note: or local area)* He knocked once.

(STEWART *knocks.)*

No answer.

(to the backstage, loudly)

He knocked again!

OLIVER. *(nasty)* Maybe this is why no one *likes* you.

CARMEN. Whoa – go on stage!

(CARMEN *pushes* **OLIVER** *toward stage.)*

ANABEL. I don't get why he's so upset!

CARMEN. Isn't it obvious? Oliver is SO jealous of you.

MAX. He knocked again!

*(Onstage. **OLIVER** enters.)*

STEWART. Oh. Hello beautiful creature, Were you by any chance at the King's Ball last night?

OLIVER. *(over it)* Yes I was there and I saw everything.

STEWART. Uh…might you have left your slipper? It belongs to the woman who is to be my bride.

(sings)

I'LL TRY ON THIS SLIPPER

OLIVER. It's not gonna fit me.

STEWART.

SEE IF IT FITS HER

OLIVER. Do we really have to do this?

STEWART.

AND SHE WILL BE MY PRINCESS…

*(**OLIVER** sticks his foot out, **STEWART** gamely tries it on, it doesn't fit, pulls out an empty 40 bottle awkwardly.)*

OLIVER. Guess it wasn't meant to be. Too bad.

*(**OLIVER** exits to backstage.)*

ANABEL. Oliver, what's your problem?

OLIVER. Don't even talk to me.

CARMEN. Stewart and Anabel didn't do anything wrong! She's just excited that she's finally had her first kiss.

ANABEL. What? Carmen, seriously?

OLIVER. *(mockingly)* Oh, never been kissed, huh? Wah wah, go suck a dick.

CARMEN. Oh, she hasn't done that yet!

ANABEL. Carmen!

OLIVER. Ha. Little Anabel's just waiting for the right time huh?

ANABEL. *(frustrated)* Well at least my boy is honest with me!

CARMEN. What?

(onstage)

MAX. The Prince found the second stepsister.

(backstage)

CARMEN. Wait what are you talking about, Anabel?

(onstage)

MAX. The second stepsister!

*(**CARMEN** enters onstage. **OLIVER** exits other way.)*

STEWART. Hello fair maiden.

(sings)

MAY I TRY ON THIS –

CARMEN. That's not my shoe.

STEWART.

SEE IF IT FITS HER?

CARMEN. Max, what are you not telling me?

STEWART.

AND SHE WILL BE MY PRINCESS…

*(**MAX** gestures "not now." **ANABEL** enters.)*

ANABEL. Hark! Oh hello, I did not know we had royal company in our humble homestead.

STEWART. *(sings)*

MAY I TRY ON THIS SLIPPER?

*(**OLIVER** enters the scene, disgusted.)*

OLIVER. *(sings)*

I'M SURE IT WILL FIT HER

*(**ANABEL** tries on the boot, it fits.)*

STEWART.

AND NOW I'M SUPPOSED TO KISS HER…

*(**ANABEL** looks at **OLIVER**, in a "oh God, this is going to make things worse" kind of way. She takes out her Invisalign, sucks in saliva and kisses **STEWART**.)*

OLIVER. *(bitter)* Congratulations.

*(**OLIVER** exits.)*

MAX. And everyone lived happily ever after.
Phew.

(Unseen campers boo.)

STEWART. Shut up!
Everyone follow me to arts and crafts.

*(**STEWART** exits. **ANABEL** starts cleaning up onstage.)*

CARMEN. Not so fast. What are you hiding? Anabel said
you're not being honest with me.

MAX. She said what?

(beat)

ANABEL. Max, I'm sorry! But remember what you told me
about trusting people! You have to tell her!

CARMEN. Tell me what!?

MAX. Can we go talk about this somewhere else?

CARMEN. I'm not going anywhere. Tell me what you're talking about.

MAX. I...don't know how to say this, there's a girl at home...

CARMEN. *(getting angry)* What? You have a girlfriend?

MAX. No, Carmen, she's not my girlfriend. But she's pregnant. And I'm the father.

(blackout)

(end of Scene Twelve)

Scene Thirteen

(INT. BUNK)

(**CARMEN** *is sitting on her bed, looking at pictures of her brother while she's on the phone with her Mom.*)

CARMEN. Yes, I'm eating. Yes, everything's fine. No, really, it's fine.

(beat)

Mom, I really just can't deal with you crying right now. We all miss him. I...I have to go. I love you.

(**CARMEN** *hangs up. Music starts – "**SHINE**")*

(sings)

DEEP BREATH, CLOSE YOUR EYES
CONJURE UP THE SKIES
STILLNESS IN THE AIR
THERE ARE STORIES YET TO SHARE
OUR LIVES ARE INTERTWINED
LIKE THE STARS ABOVE, ALIGNED

THERE'S A CONSTELLATION OF SEVEN STARS
WITH RELATIONSHIPS JUST LIKE OURS
FLUNG TOGETHER IN SOME PLAN
THAT WE'RE NOT MEANT TO UNDERSTAND
I LOOK UP AND WONDER WHY
JUST SIX LIGHT UP THE SKY

TELL ME HOW DOES THAT SEVENTH STAR GET THROUGH
   THE NIGHT?
SHE'S ALL ALONE, AND SHE'S TREMBLING WITH FRIGHT
NO ONE CAN SEE HER SPIRIT SHINE BRIGHT
BUT JUST BELIEVE IT

MAYBE THE SKY IS COVERED IN DUST
OR MAYBE YOUR EYES ARE BETRAYING YOUR TRUST
KEEP THEM BOTH OPEN AND ONE DAY YOU'LL SEE
HER SHINE
WITH ME

CARMEN. *(cont.)*

> I PUT MY TRUST IN WHAT FELT RIGHT
> I LET HIM IN WITHOUT A FIGHT
> HE'S KEEPING SECRETS HERE AND THERE
> I'M CONVENIENTLY LEFT UNAWARE
> I'VE GOT TO GATHER UP MY PRIDE
> AND REMIND MYSELF, HE LIED
>
> TELL ME HOW CAN ANYONE GET THROUGH THE NIGHT?
> CONSCIOUSLY KEEPING THINGS HIDDEN FROM SIGHT
> WHERE CAN YOU FIND THE COURAGE TO FIGHT
> WHEN YOU FEEL BROKEN?
>
> MAYBE THE DARKNESS IS HIDING HER FACE
> OR MAYBE SHE'S TRYING BUT FALLING FROM GRACE
> WAIT WITH COMPASSION AND ONE DAY YOU'LL SEE
> HER SHINE
> AND SHINE
>
> STRONG AND RESOLUTE
> YOU'LL MAKE IT THROUGH THIS
> GATHER ALL YOUR DIGNITY AND
> SCREW THIS
> PLACE
> AND SCREW THIS GUY
> ABOVE, HER LIGHT STARTS TO DIE
>
> MAYBE THE LIGHT COMES FROM SOMEWHERE INSIDE
> IT'S BURSTING WITH LOVE THAT CANNOT BE DENIED
> MAYBE TOMORROW I'LL LOOK UP TO SEE
> HER SHINE
> AND SHINE
> WITH ME

(Song ends. **MAX** *enters tentatively.)*

MAX. Carmen? Can we talk about this?

CARMEN. Just go away. *(incredulous)* You got someone pregnant, thought it was a good idea to hide it from me, and now want me to sympathize?

MAX. See, this is exactly why we shouldn't have gotten involved, none of this is fair to you.

> *(beat)*

Look, I just need you to know that she is just a friend,
we were never dating. We were drunk, and I know
that's not an excuse, but we were just fooling around.
We have no romantic feelings at all, either of us.

(beat)

But now I'm going to be a father.

CARMEN. What are you going to do? Are you going to help
raise it?

MAX. Of course I am! It's...my reality. And I'm going to
take responsibility. But I never expected to fall for you.

CARMEN. Why didn't you just tell me? It's all very shady, Max.

MAX. I didn't tell you because I just found out a few weeks
ago, and she wasn't even sure what she was going to do.
I told her I would respect any decision that she made,
but I was just waiting to see what was going to happen.

(pause)

You know when you don't say something, and then it
kind of snowballs until you don't even know how to
bring it up?

CARMEN. Max, I think it's...great that you're going to do
what's right. But you can't just keep things inside like
this.

(beat)

My brother kept things bottled up inside, and then it
was too late for me to help him.

MAX. (confused) What are you talking about?

CARMEN. My brother killed himself a few months ago. He
felt like he couldn't talk to anyone. Max, I know that
you're freaked out, and what you're going through is
difficult, but not talking about it and not accepting
help is only going to make it harder.

(CARMEN places her hand on MAX's.)

You know I'm on your side, right?

MAX. I can't. No, no, I fucked this up too much already. I
don't even deserve to be with someone like you.

(**MAX** *starts to leave, forgetting his journal.*)

CARMEN. Max!

(**MAX** *stops.*)

MAX. Carmen! I just can't.

(**MAX** *exits.* **CARMEN** *picks up his journal. Music starts – "NEVER DOUBT MY LOVE"*)

CARMEN.

AND I
DON'T KNOW HOW TO DO THIS
I'VE TRIED SO HARD
WHAT CAN I DO TO SHOW YOU
NEVER DOUBT MY LOVE?

DOUBT THAT THE STARS ARE ON FIRE
DOUBT THAT THE SUN DOTH MOVE
DOUBT TRUTH TO BE A LIAR
BUT NEVER DOUBT MY LOVE

(**MAX** *enters in the side.*)

CARMEN & MAX.

DOUBT THAT THE STARS ARE ON FIRE
DOUBT THAT THE SUN DOTH MOVE
DOUBT TRUTH TO BE A LIAR
BUT NEVER DOUBT MY LOVE

(**OLIVER** *enters in on the side.*)

CARMEN, MAX & OLIVER.

DOUBT THAT THE STARS ARE ON FIRE
DOUBT THAT THE SUN DOTH MOVE
DOUBT TRUTH TO BE A LIAR
BUT NEVER DOUBT MY LOVE

(**ANABEL** *and* **STEWART** *enter.*)

ALL 5.

DOUBT THAT THE STARS ARE ON FIRE
DOUBT THAT THE SUN DOTH MOVE
DOUBT TRUTH TO BE A LIAR
BUT NEVER DOUBT MY LOVE
NEVER DOUBT MY LOVE

(Song ends.)

(Lights down on **CARMEN**, **MAX**, *and* **OLIVER**, *leaving* **STEWART** *and* ANABEL *onstage.)*

STEWART. Hey there, Cinderella.

ANABEL. Hi, my noble prince.

STEWART. Are you ok?

ANABEL. I don't know, I've never seen Oliver this upset... except when I broke his Lucille Ball figurine. But that's another story...and then what I did to Max, I just hate feeling like I'm hurting people...

STEWART. It's not your fault. Let's keep this in perspective: this is summer camp. We all have bigger things ahead of us. You know, what I said in the play, about exploring this "magnificent world together"...I think we should do that.

ANABEL. What?

STEWART. Life's too short to just... I mean... Look at Max... Who knows where we'll be in a year...

ANABEL. Well I'll be in school, at Notre Dame.

STEWART. Screw Notre Dame! Screw college! Let's get out of here!

ANABEL. What are you talking about?

STEWART. *(passionately)* This isn't ME. I feel like I've been driving down this one fucking road my whole life, and I don't even know where it's going or if I want to go there. And honestly, I don't want to end up in the middle of nowhere studying something I don't care about just to make my parents happy!

*(Music Starts – "**TAKE THIS CHANCE**")*

I have to get away from everything
for a while.

Come with me!

(sings)

BACKPACKS ON
NALGENES FULL
SUN RISING OVERHEAD

STEWART.

> TAKE THE PLUNGE
> LOOK AROUND
> SOME GYPSIES UP AHEAD!

ANABEL. They're called the Romany people.

STEWART.

> A WHOLE OTHER WORLD THAT EXISTED
> COME WITH ME NOW,
> HOLD MY HAND
>
> TAKE THIS CHANCE
> WE'LL DO IT TOGETHER
> YOU AND I
> CARS, TRAINS AND BUSES
> THIS CHANCE
> MILE AFTER MILE
> THE FUTURE IS IN YOUR HANDS
> THROW AWAY ALL YOUR PLANS
> AND TAKE THIS CHANCE

ANABEL. No, seriously, you can't call them Gypsies, it's a thing. And Stewart –

STEWART.

> THE LONDON EYE
> TRAFALGAR SQUARE
> TACKY TOURIST KITSCH

ANABEL. London's dirty, Stewart.

STEWART.

> RAINS ALL DAY
> THE HOSTEL SMELLS
> EXCHANGE RATE IS A BITCH

ANABEL. I really don't want to share a bathroom!

STEWART.

> BUT EUROPE WOULD BE AN ADVENTURE
> COME WITH ME NOW
> WAIT YOU'LL SEE
>
> TAKE THIS CHANCE
> WE'LL DO IT TOGETHER

YOU AND I
AIRPLANES AND VESPAS
THIS CHANCE
MILE AFTER MILE
THE FUTURE IS IN YOUR HANDS
THROW AWAY ALL YOUR PLANS
AND TAKE THIS CHANCE

ANABEL. Stewart, you're way ahead of yourself!

STEWART. Come on, think about how much fun we'd have!

ANABEL. Yeah it could be fun, but I can't make that decision right now! I just need some time…

(**ANABEL** *runs out.*)

STEWART.

THE TIME IS NOW
MY PARENTS LOSE THEIR GOLDEN CHILD
WAIT AND THEY'LL SEE
WHAT I CAN BE!
WHAT I CAN BE!

TAKE THIS CHANCE
WITH NO EXPECTATIONS
ON THE ROAD
I'LL WALK IF I HAVE TO
THIS CHANCE
MILE AFTER MILE
THE FUTURE IS IN MY HANDS
FOLLOWING NO ONE'S PLANS
I'LL TAKE THIS CHANCE

I'LL TAKE THIS CHANCE

(*Lights down.*)

(*end of Scene Thirteen*)

Scene Fourteen

(Exterior - dock)

*(**MAX** enters onto the dock, upset. Music starts –
"**SELFISHLY**")*

MAX. *(sings)*
WHEN A TREE FALLS IN THE WOODS
AND NO ONE IS AROUND
DOES IT EVEN MATTER
HOW HARD IT HITS THE GROUND?

CAN A BOY PURSUE A GIRL
DESPITE ALL COMMON SENSE
KNOWING THAT HIS DAYS ARE NUMBERED,
PROCEDING AT HER EXPENSE?

AND IT'S NOT FAIR
AND IT'S NOT RIGHT
THERE'S NO TIME TO SPARE
I'M JUST SO SCARED
I'VE GOT TO STAND AND FIGHT

CAUSE IT'S NOT ABOUT ME
OH NO, NO
SHE DESERVES BETTER THAN ME
I GUARANTEE
THAT I WON'T BE THE ONE
TO TAKE HER HEART AND BREAK IT
SELFISHLY

AND SHE NEEDS
SOMEONE STRONG, SOMEONE WHO CAN BE
THERE FOR HER
WHO WOULD EXCEED
HER EXPECTATIONS
SHE NEEDS
SOMEONE
ANYONE BETTER THAN ME

MAX. *(cont.)*

AH
NO
AH
NO

NO I CAN'T BE THE ONE
AND SHE WON'T BE THE ONE
NO I WON'T BE THE ONE
TO TAKE HER HEART
BREAK HER HEART
I'LL FORSAKE MY HEART
SELFISHLY

(End song.)

(end of Scene Fourteen)

Scene Fifteen

(Interior - Bunk)

(OLIVER *is throwing a ball against the wall, pensively.*
ANABEL *comes in slowly.)*

ANABEL. Hey.

OLIVER. Hey.

ANABEL. I didn't know you saw me and Stewart kissing and I'm really sorry.

OLIVER. It's fine. He obviously likes you.

ANABEL. Yeah, but you like him too. I shouldn't have stepped on your toes.

OLIVER. Why are you always sorry for being yourself? I was just jealous.

ANABEL. Jealous of what? You know I don't know what I'm doing.

OLIVER. Anabel, you always win everything. It's not even that Stewart didn't like me – lots of guys don't like me. It's that once again, you come out on top.

ANABEL. Oliver, I've wanted to be like you my whole life! While I was at home studying, you were out living! Yeah I had a crush on Stewart, but what made it exciting was that for the first time, someone liked me back.

OLIVER. *(teasing)* So, what? You have a boyfriend now?

ANABEL. Haha, no I don't think so. But I'm glad he made me feel like I could if I wanted to. And I'd like to visit you in New York, IF you promise not to make a video blog about it!

OLIVER. Haha I won't, you're not very photogenic anyway.

ANABEL. Shut up!

(They hug, music starts for "Love Always, Me," **ANABEL**
goes to her bed to start writing in her journal, **OLIVER**
gets his video camera out and prepares to video blog.)

*(Song starts: "**LOVE ALWAYS, ME**")*

ANABEL. *(cont.)* *(sings)*
> DEAR DIARY
> YOU MIGHT AGREE
> IT'S BEEN A CRAZY PAST TWO WEEKS
> SO MUCH HAS CHANGED
> THAT I COULD SCREAM
>
> MY CARDIGAN
> FELL APART AGAIN
> I GUESS IT WASN'T MEANT TO BE
> THE FABRIC'S
> BURSTING AT THE SEAM
>
> BUT ALL THE WHILE
> I CAN'T HELP BUT SMILE
> BECAUSE I'VE NEVER FELT
> THIS WAY
> BEFORE
>
> CAN'T YOU SEE
> TO SOME DEGREE
> THAT FINALLY
> I'M NOT THE ODD ONE OUT?
>
> AND IT MAKES ME HAPPY
> LOVE ALWAYS,
> ME

*(**STEWART** walks in, writing on a notepad.)*

STEWART. *(sings)*
> DEAR MOM AND DAD
> IT MAKES ME SAD
> TO HAVE TO TELL YOU QUITE LIKE THIS
> BUT HERE I GO
> SO DON'T BE MAD
>
> SEE, HERE'S THE THING
> EVER SINCE THE SPRING
> I'VE BEEN SCRAMBLING
> TO ORGANIZE MY LIFE
> I PROMISE THIS WON'T BE THAT BAD

STEWART. *(cont.)*

> THERE'S SOMETHING I
> GOTTA DO BEFORE I DIE
> BECAUSE I'VE NEVER FELT
> THIS WAY
> BEFORE
>
> CAN'T YOU SEE
> TO SOME DEGREE
> I'VE GOTTA BE
> FREE TO DISAGREE
>
> AND I WANNA BE HAPPY
> LOVE ALWAYS,
> ME

ANABEL.

> BEST SUMMER EVER
> OH YEAH
> DOO DOO DOO DOO…

STEWART.

> HOW DO I SAY THIS?
> I'M OBVIOUSLY WHIPPED BY MY DAD
> HOW DO I DO THIS?
> HE'S GONNA BE SO EFFING MAD

(Lights up on **OLIVER**, *starting his video blog.)*

OLIVER. *(sings)*

> HEY ALL MY PEEPS
> THOUGH I PLAY FOR KEEPS
> SOMETIMES MY PRIDE MUST PAY A PRICE
> WHICH BRINGS ME TO THIS SOUND ADVICE
>
> WHEN YOU LOSE THE GAME
> DON'T CONFUSE THE BLAME
> I KNOW IT'S HARD TO KEEP IT IN
> BUT DON'T PROJECT IT ON YOUR TWIN
> *(or whoever!)*
>
> AND ALL THE WHILE
> IT'LL HELP IF YOU JUST SMILE
> AND LEAVE THE PAST BEHIND

JUST CHECK YO'SELF
'FORE YOU WRECK YO'SELF
JUST TAKE A SEC YO'SELF TO CHILL
CAUSE WE DESERVE TO BE HAPPY
LOVE ALWAYS, ME

OLIVER.	ANABEL.	STEWART.
HEY ALL MY PEEPS	DEAR DIARY	DEAR MOM AND DAD
JUST LET ME SAY	YOU MIGHT AGREE	IT MAKES ME SAD
IF YOU LOSE THE GAME	IT'S BEEN A CRAZY PAST TWO WEEKS	TO TELL YOU QUITE LIKE THIS
DON'T CONFUSE THE BLAME	SO MUCH CHANGED THAT I COULD SCREAM	BUT HERE I GO
I KNOW IT'S HARD	AND I AM BURSTING AT THE SEAM	DON'T BE MAD
TO KEEP IT IN	BUT ALL THE WHILE	I PROMISE IT WON'T BE BAD
IF YOU JUST SMILE	I CAN'T HELP BUT SMILE	THERE'S SOMETHING I
NEVER FELT THIS WAY BEFORE!	BECAUSE I'VE NEVER FELT THIS WAY BEFORE!	GOTTA DO BEFORE I DIE THIS WAY BEFORE!

ALL.

CAN'T YOU SEE
TO SOME DEGREE
THAT THERE'S A SPARK INSIDE OF ME

ANABEL.

AND IT MAKES ME HAPPY

STEWART.

AND I WANNA BE HAPPY

OLIVER.

>CAUSE WE DESERVE TO BE HAPPY

ANABEL & STEWART.

>HAPPY

OLIVER. I've also snagged a new boy, but that'll have to wait until next time!

ALL.

>LOVE ALWAYS…
>ME!

(Song ends, lights down.)

(end of Scene Fifteen)

Scene Sixteen

(**MAX** *is sitting on the bleachers,* **OLIVER** *walks in with* **STEWART** *not seeing* **MAX**.)

LOUDSPEAKER. Attention all campers: please remember the rules for the end of summer dance tonight. Inappropriate dancing is defined as any below-the-belt body parts touching, but have fun...somehow!

OLIVER. *(to* **STEWART**) Ok, go stand by that tree and do what I showed you.

STEWART. God, this is so stupid.

OLIVER. *(filming)* Whatever! It's a photoshoot, just have fun!

(**OLIVER** *tries to help* **STEWART** *pose.*)

Less broken spirit, more broken doll...
Here, do it with me.

(*They both attempt "broken doll" pose.*)

(*seeing* **MAX**)

Speaking of broken spirits...

(**OLIVER** *and* **STEWART** *approach* **MAX**.)

Are you ok?

MAX. Guys, I'm fine.

STEWART. Well you can't just sit here and mope all night.

(*teasing*)

You have to get your groove on tonight at the dance! I put together a kickass playlist!

MAX. I hope that doesn't include Yanni: Live at the Acropolis...

STEWART. Hey! Don't make fun of the Yan-ster!

OLIVER. Max! Snap out of it! It's about Carmen, am I wrong? You're still going to the dance with her tonight, right? We're leaving tomorrow. It's your last chance.

(*Music starts* "**LIFE'S TOO SHORT/OPEN YOUR HEART.**")

MAX. I don't even know if it's worth it.

OLIVER. Shut up, why wouldn't it be worth it?

STEWART. You know life's way too short to just sit around and wait for things to happen to you!

STEWART. *(sings)*

AT SIX YEARS OLD
I WAS KING OF THE SANDBOX
NO ONE QUESTIONED MY RULE
EVERY RECESS FROM TWELVE UNTIL TWELVE THIRTY
ACTING UNDISPUTEDLY CRUEL

MOCKING AND TAUNTING, TIL RICKY WAILS
PULLING ABBY'S PIGTAILS
A SHOVEL MY SCEPTER,
BUCKET MY CROWN
NO ONE'S GONNA BRING ME DOWN!

BUT THEN MY LIFE
THREW ME A CURVEBALL
CHICKEN POX, MEASLES AND ALL
MY REIGN WAS OVER
WITH JUST ONE HOSPITAL BAND
BUT LIFE'S TOO SHORT
TO CRY OVER SAND!

(Scene shifts. **CARMEN** *and* **ANABEL** *are getting ready for the camp dance.)*

ANABEL. I know this dance is supposed to be for the kids, but I'm so excited! Hey, can I borrow your Bumpit tonight?

CARMEN. Shhh, don't talk about my Bumpit. But yeah, here, I don't need it anyway.

ANABEL. Ah, this is so cool!

CARMEN. It doesn't take a lot to excite you, does it?

ANABEL. I'm just really looking forward to tonight. It's like everything has been leading up to this.

CARMEN. Yeah, don't remind me…

ANABEL. *(sings)*

> DO YOU LIKE THIS DRESS?
> I NEED A DRESS THAT SAYS
> THIS GIRL IS HOT
> AND YOU HAVEN'T GOT A SHOT
>
> DO YOU LIKE MY HAIR?
> I COULD WEAR IT UP OR LET IT DOWN
> I FEEL LIKE SUCH A CLOWN
>
> BUT WHAT MATTERS
> IS THAT YOU FEEL SEXY
> AND ASSURED
>
> *(tarting up* **CARMEN** *)*
>
> NOT SO DEMURE!
>
> JUST OPEN YOUR HEART
> THERE'S JUST ONE NIGHT
> TO TELL HIM HOW YOU FEEL
> SO PUT YOUR FACE ON
> GRAB THOSE FOUR-INCH HEELS
> JUST SEAL THE DEAL!
> TIME WILL REVEAL HOW HE FEELS
> JUST OPEN YOUR HEART
>
> *(Scene shifts back to boys.)*

MAX. Touching story, Stewart, but this isn't kid stuff, this is my LIFE!

> **(OLIVER***'s phone rings, he quickly looks and ignores it.)*

OLIVER. Bitch please, Clear the stage!

> *(sings)*
>
> BOY SOPRANO
> AT TWELVE YEARS OLD
> SINGING FLAWLESSLY BRIGHT
> (OOOH!)
> CHRISTMAS CONCERT
> I'M READY FOR THAT SOLO
> GONNA SING MY ASS OFF TONIGHT

OLIVER. *(cont.)*
    CURTAIN RISES
    STRIKE UP THE BAND
    MAESTRO LIFT YOUR HAND
    OPEN MY MOUTH TO
    LET IT OUT
    BELTING OUT WITHOUT A DOUBT!

    BUT THEN MY LIFE
    THREW ME A CURVEBALL
    MY VOICE CRACKED ALL THROUGH THE HALL!
    I WAS A TENOR, SHIT!
    IN JUST ONE DROP OF THE BALL
    BUT LIFE'S TOO SHORT
    TO CRY WHEN YOU FALL!

    (Scene switches back to girls.)

CARMEN. But Anabel, Max TOLD me he didn't want to pursue anything.

ANABEL. That doesn't mean you should just give up on him! Just go tonight and see what happens, what do you have to lose?

CARMEN. Everything!

    (sings)

    DO YOU LIKE THIS HUGE SWEATSTAIN?
    I NEED A TISSUE!
    MY STRAP KEEPS FALLING DOWN
    GOD, I FEEL LIKE SUCH A CLOWN

ANABEL. *(deadpan)* You really have to pull yourself together.

CARMEN.
    LOOK INTO MY EYES
    I'M SO NERVOUS
    I FEEL LIKE I COULD DIE

ANABEL. Nobody's gonna die!

CARMEN. Oh shut up!

ANABEL. You're ridic.

(**ANABEL** *hands* **CARMEN** *a tissue.*)

BUT WHAT MATTERS
IS THE HERE AND NOW
AND THE COURAGE TO CARRY ON
BEFORE WE'RE GONE

JUST OPEN YOUR HEART
THERE'S JUST ONE NIGHT
TO TELL HIM HOW YOU FEEL
SO HERE'S SOME LIPGLOSS
GRAB THOSE FOUR-INCH HEELS
JUST SEAL THE DEAL!
TIME WILL REVEAL HOW HE FEELS
JUST OPEN YOUR HEART

CARMEN.

OPEN MY HEART
HOW I FEEL

Thanks.

(*Light on both scenes now.*)

CARMEN & MAX.

WE HAVE SUCH LITTLE TIME
TO DO THE THINGS WE WANT TO
IN THIS LIFE

ANABEL & STEWART.

SO THROW YOUR HAT INTO THE RING

ANABEL & OLIVER.

INSTEAD OF WAITING IN THE WINGS

CARMEN & MAX.

IT'S DO OR DIE
I CAN'T BE SHY
I NEED THE COURAGE JUST TO TRY

ANABEL, STEWART & OLIVER.

JUST TRY

ALL 5.

I!

CARMEN & MAX.
     WILL SEE
ANABEL, STEWART, OLIVER.
     YOU'LL SEE
ALL 5.
     TONIGHT!

     (Music interlude under. **OLIVER***'s phone rings.)*

STEWART. Who keeps calling you?

OLIVER. Nobody!

ANABEL.
     WITH AN OPEN HEART
     AND AN OPEN MIND
     AND OPEN LEGS YOU'LL FIND!
STEWART & OLIVER.
     THAT WHEN LIFE
     THROWS YOU A CURVEBALL
     BETTER BE THERE READY TO HIT
STEWART.
     YOUR GIRL IS WAITING
OLIVER.
     SO KEEP THAT FIRE LIT
THE GIRLS.
     OPEN YOUR HEART
     THERE'S JUST ONE NIGHT
THE BOYS.
     CAUSE LIFE'S TOO SHORT TO MOPE
THE GIRLS.
     TIME WILL REVEAL HOW HE FEELS
THE BOYS.
     AND LIFE'S TOO SHORT TO WHINE
THE GIRLS.
     TIME WILL REVEAL HOW HE FEELS
THE BOYS.
     AND LIFE'S TOO SHORT
ALL.
     TO CRY OVER IT!
     DON'T CRY OVER IT!

(Lights down on girls. Oliver's phone rings again.)

MAX. Seriously, answer it.

LOUDSPEAKER. Attention: will Oliver please answer his phone?

*(**MAX** and **STEWART** look at each other.)*

STEWART. You're friends with the gay loudspeaker?

MAX. Of course he's friends with the gay loudspeaker.

OLIVER. Well, not exactly friends…

LOUDSPEAKER. Attention: I can hear you.

OLIVER. *(loudly, so **LOUDSPEAKER** can hear)* WE'VE BEEN DATING FOR THE PAST 2 WEEKS. Ever since I went to to the office to raid the care packages. I didn't want you guys to find out because…it's weird.

STEWART. *(mocking **OLIVER**)* Oh my God, where's your camera? We need to document this precipitous turn of events.

OLIVER. You're a precipitous.

MAX. Look at us. We are all weird.

*(**ANABEL** comes saunterprancing in, **OLIVER** films her and she postures for the camera.)*

ANABEL. Hi guys! Am I tardy for the party?

OLIVER. Gross, I just vomited all over myself.

ANABEL. Haha whatever, people say that.

MAX. *(to unseen campers)* Hey boys! No grinding on the dance floor!

STEWART. You look nice. Is that your real hair?

ANABEL. It's Carmen's Bumpit. Oops, I wasn't supposed to talk about it.

MAX. Where is Carmen?

ANABEL. Oh, she's coming. Max, don't fuck it up.

STEWART. The new Anabel swears too?

OLIVER. The new Anabel does a lot of things.

*(Music starts – "**FINALE**.")*

(**OLIVER** *starts filming* **STEWART** *and* **ANABEL**.)

ANABEL. When do you leave for your trip?

STEWART. As soon as possible. I'm talking to my parents tomorrow...and, we'll see how they take it.

OLIVER. Good, I'm glad you decided to tell them, and I'm going to hold you to it cause I got it all on film!

ANABEL. Oh my god guys, this is it! Our last night together!

ANABEL.
THIS SUMMER FLEW BY SO FAST

STEWART.
OUR TIME HERE WON'T GO UNSURPASSED

OLIVER.
THE TIME HAS PASSED
I HAD A BLAST
AND WANT THE MEMORIES TO LAST

MAX.
OUR LAST NIGHT
THE STONE'S BEEN CAST
WE'LL MOVE ON WITH LIFE
THE WORLD SO VAST
OUTWIT, OUTPLAY
AND STILL OUTLAST
I'LL OUTLAST

ALL 4.
LIVE TO LOVE
LOVE TO LIVE
LIFE'S TOO SHORT
TO NOT FORGIVE
WITH NO REGRETS
LIVE FOR TODAY
JUST DAY BY DAY

(**CARMEN** *enters slowly.* **MAX** *sees her, his eyes light up.*
ANABEL *pushes* **MAX** *towards* **CARMEN**.)

ANABEL, STEWART, OLIVER. *(under)*
LIVE TO LOVE
LOVE TO LIVE
LIVE TO LOVE
LOVE TO LIVE

MAX. Carmen…if you're willing to try…

CARMEN. Max. Of course I am.

    *(**MAX** and **CARMEN** hug.)*

MAX. Look! Seven stars.

CARMEN.
    I NEVER THOUGHT
    I'D FALL SO HARD
    MY FEELINGS FOR YOU
    CAUGHT ME OFF GUARD

MAX.
    JUST LIVE FOR TODAY
    WE'LL FIND A WAY

MAX & CARMEN.
    DAY BY DAY

ALL 5.
    LIVE TO LOVE
    LOVE TO LIVE
    LIFE'S TOO SHORT
    TO NOT FORGIVE
    WITH NO REGRETS
    LIVE FOR TODAY
    JUST DAY BY DAY

ALL 4.	**CARMEN.**
LIVE TO LOVE	AND I
LOVE TO LIVE	HOPE THAT I CAN DO THIS
LIFE'S TOO SHORT	I'M READY TO LEARN
TO NOT FORGIVE	WATCH AND YOU'LL SEE
WITH NO REGRETS	THAT I'M
LIVE FOR TODAY	WORKING TOWARD
	TOMORROW
JUST DAY BY DAY	I'M READY TO GIVE

ALL 4.	CARMEN.
LIVE TO LOVE	AND I
LOVE TO LIVE	DON'T KNOW HOW TO DO THIS
LIFE'S TOO SHORT	I'M READY TO LEARN
TO NOT FORGIVE	WATCH AND YOU'LL SEE
WITH NO REGRETS	THAT I'M
LIVE FOR TODAY	WORKING TOWARD TOMORROW
JUST DAY BY DAY	I'M READY TO LIVE

ALL 5. *(5 part counterpoint)*

OOO LIVE TO LOVE
OOO LOVE TO LIVE
OOO WITH NO REGRETS
OOO AND DON'T LOOK BACK

LOVE
LIVE TO LOVE
LIVE FOR TODAY

JUST DAY BY DAY
LIVE
TO
LOVE!

End

OTHER TITLES AVAILABLE FROM SAMUEL FRENCH

FUNNY BUSINESS

Book by Rachel Brittain and Daniel Falk
Music and Lyrics by Daniel Abrahamson

Comedy / 3m, 2f

When low morale threatens the Toronto branch of Chime Communications Canada, five ordinary office workers must mount a team-building talent show to savetheir jobs. Meet Stuart, the lovable yet inappropriate office manager, Marcus, the smooth talking sales rep, Diane, the tough as nails marketing manager, Brie, the perky and scheming receptionist, and Jack, the awkward guitar-playing intern. Together, they must use their hidden talents to sing, dance and manipulate their way through the talent show, which ultimately degenerates into a every-man-for-themselves battle of office skills, where only one will walk away without a pink slip. Featuring a sales versus marketing salsa, a fowl-mouthed printer puppet, and more office backstabbing than HR can handle, the team must learn to keep it together without tearing each other apart.

This fast-paced, comedic romp through office culture features a catchy, original pop-musical score, and five unforgettable characters that you're bound to recognize from around the water cooler. An exciting and fun new musical, *Funny Business* is the perfect production for cubicle dwellers and blue collars alike.

Fresh, tuneful, and full of talent…a guaranteed good time!"
– *Toronto Star*

"Brilliant musical comedy!"
– *NOW Magazine*

"Four stars! A breakout success!"
– *EYE Weekly*

OTHER TITLES AVAILABLE FROM SAMUEL FRENCH

SEE ROCK CITY AND OTHER DESTINATIONS

Book & Lyrics by Adam Mathias
Music by Brad Alexander

4m, 3f expandable to 7m, 6f / Simple Set

**WINNER! 2011 Drama Desk Award for
Outstanding Book, Adam Mathias!**

See Rock City & Other Destinations is a contemporary musical about connections missed and made at tourist destinations across America.

A wanderer believes his destiny is written on rooftops along the North Carolina Interstate. A young man yearns to connect with intelligent life in Roswell, New Mexico. A woman at the Alamo steps out of the shadow of her grandparents' idealized romance to take a chance on love. Three estranged sisters cruise to Glacier Bay to scatter their father's ashes. Two high school boys face unexpected fears in the Coney Island Spook House. A terrified bride-to-be ponders taking the leap...over Niagara Falls.

With a score that incorporates pop, rock, folk and more, each story builds on the last to create a vivid travelogue of Americans learning to overcome their fears and expectations in order to connect.

"[See Rock City & Other Destinations] turns out to be an excellent and moving new musical... It's also beautiful, it's hopeful, and it's - in the best sense of the word - sweet."
– Jesse Oxfeld, *The New York Observer*

"The music by Brad Alexander with lyrics by Mathias is consistently lovely. The songs are polished and catchy displaying the composers' gift for writing tunes that are both versatile and genuinely moving."
– Roma Torre, NY1

OTHER TITLES AVAILABLE FROM SAMUEL FRENCH

THE BOMB-ITTY OF ERRORS

Jordan Allen-Dutton, Jason Catalano, Gregory J. Qaiyum, Erik Weiner and Jeffrey Qaiyum

Comedy with Music / 4 - 20 actors (male or female)

The Bomb-itty of Errors is an Ad-Rap-Tation, hip-hop theatre retelling of Shakespeare's *The Comedy of Errors*. It was nominated for Best Lyrics at the Drama Desk Awards, nominated for Outer Critics Circle Awards, and received the Jefferson Award in Chicago and the Grand Jury Prize at the HBO US Comedy Arts Festival in Aspen.

The show lasts one hour and thirty minutes and is part play and part rap concert.

"This energetic twist on Shakespeare's *The Comedy of Errors* is
a thrill, GRADE: A!"
– *Entertainment Weekly*

"This fantastic show is one of the most entertaining, slick and inventive you'll see on the Fringe this year—and it has some clever insights to shed on the Bard's classic farce too. Does what so many productions fail to do—it makes Shakespeare funny. Not just chuck-ling, yes-I-see-this-part-is-meant-to-be-comical funny, but laugh out loud, hollering and cheering funny. The language is as clever, sharp and twisty as Shakespeare's."
– *Edinburgh Evening News*

"A rap version of Shakespeare's *Comedy of Errors* that pulses with wit, savvy and a sublime sense of its own ridiculousness. You'll
be enchanted."
– *The Telegraph*

THE PEOPLE VS. MONA

Jim Wann and Patricia Miller

Musical / 3m, 5f (w/ doubling; expandable casting options) / Unit Set

The People vs. Mona is a love story, murder mystery, courtroom shenanigans, fate-of-a-small-town-hanging-on-the-verdict musical.

For professional companies: seven actor/singers play all the roles in a multicultural cast, accompanied by three onstage musicians. For high schools, colleges, and community theatre: the cast may be expanded by having one actor in each witness role, and a chorus of townspeople in the larger numbers.

The music combines folk, blues, gospel, jazz, rock, musical comedy, school anthem, marching band and bossa nova with a theatrical sensibility.

Mona Mae Katt, a third-generation Latina-American, owns the Frog Pad, the long-time musical heart of Tippo, GA, a town in need of a plan to revive itself. She is accused of killing C.C. Katt, recording studio operator and her husband of ten hours, by hitting him over the head with her Stratocaster guitar. She is defended by Jim Summerford, a Southern gentleman who's never won a case against prosecutor and Mayoral candidate Mavis Frye—his fiancé.

As Jim tries to prove Mona's innocence, he becomes attracted to her, and Mavis ups the stakes: she wants to convict Mona, marry Jim, take office, tear down the Frog Pad, and put up a Casino—bringing in bucks, but taking away Tippo's artistic and social traditions in the process. And if Mona is found guilty, the odds are Mavis will get her way.

Several of the actors play multiple roles in a parade of witnesses on the way to a sequence of surprise endings. *MONA* manages to combine a love triangle, courtroom drama, and character-driven comedy in an original book musical, with a light-hearted message about the importance of cultural heritage in America's towns. Keep the Frog Pad alive!